IT'S
SO
QUIET

IT'S SO QUIET

A Not-Quite-Going-to-Bed Book

by **Sherri Duskey Rinker**

illustrated by **Tony Fucile**

chronicle books san francisco

Down,
down,
down,
the sun drops behind the hill.
The farm is falling quiet.
Everything is still.

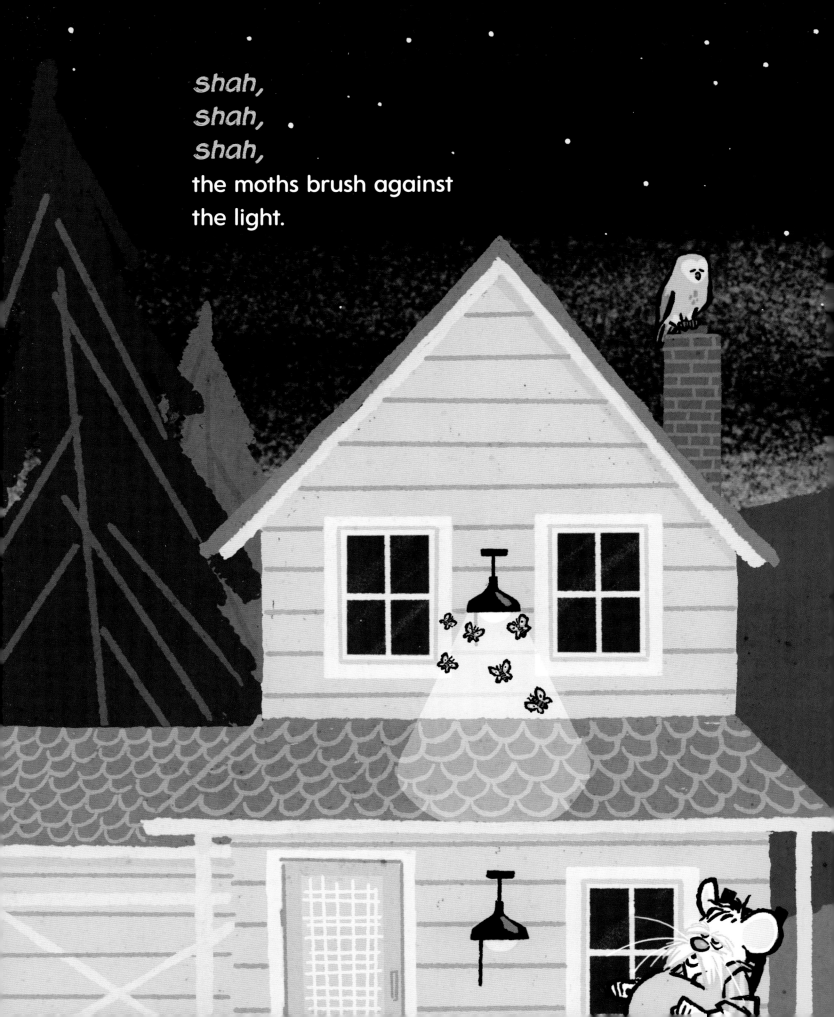

shah,
shah,
shah,
the moths brush against
the light.

A *click!* turns the lamp off.
Now there's nothing
but the night.

It's *soooo* quiet.

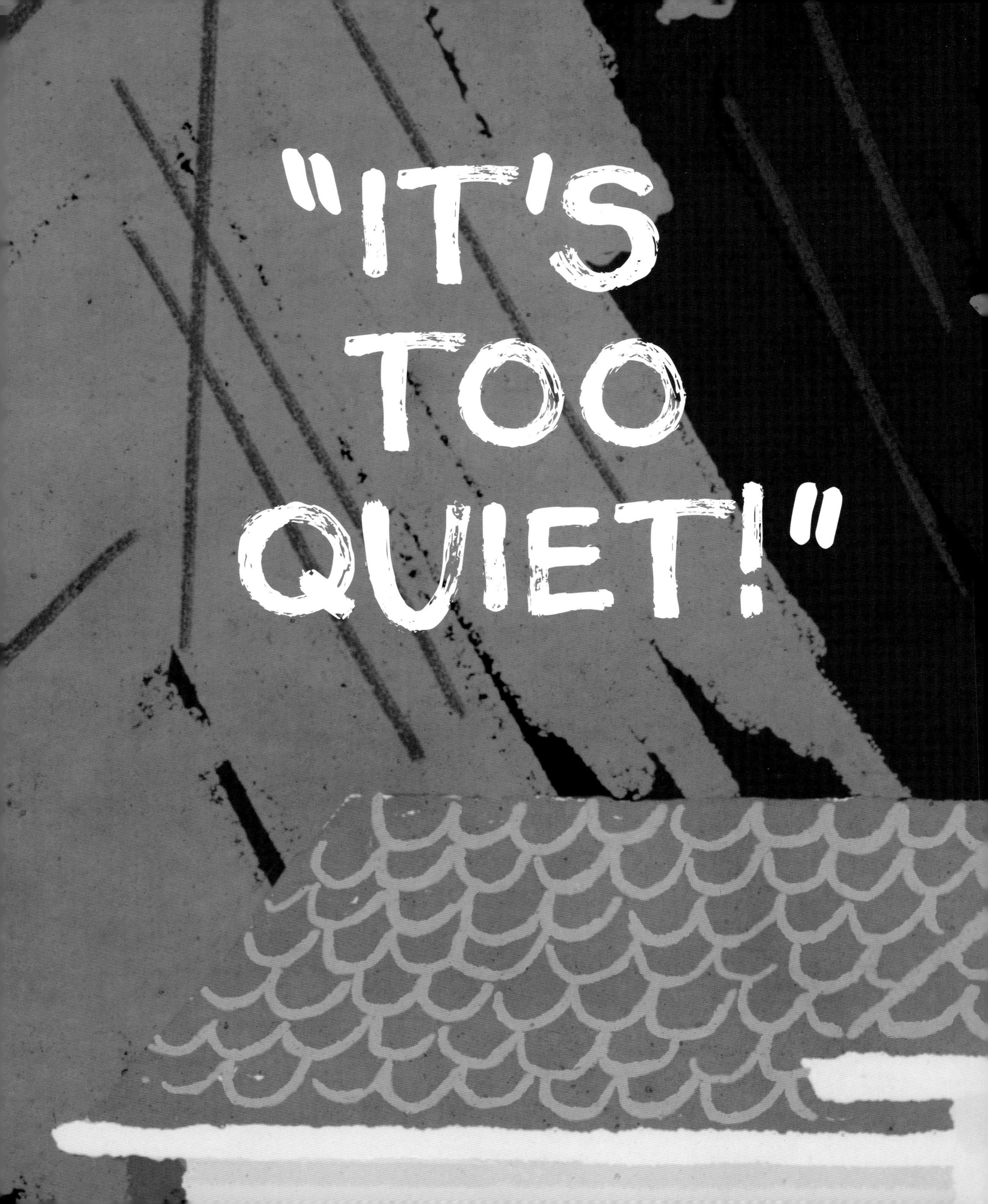
"IT'S TOO QUIET!"

In a little bed, in the little house
is a sleepy mama and a very *sleepless* mouse.

"Hush," says his mama.
"Settle down now, not a peep.
The small sweet sounds of nighttime
will whisper you to sleep . . .

. . . listen."

crrr-oak,
crrr-oak,
bullfrog sings through the thickets.

chirp chirp,
chirp chirp,
chime in all the crickets.

squeeeal,
rat-tat-tat,
blows the old screen door.

tip-tap,
tip-tap,
hound dog's tail beats the floor.

wwwwwhooooosssssshhhhh,

sings the breeze, through the trees.

snort!
bloop-bloop-bloop,

that's Granddad's snore.

snort!
bloop-bloop-bloop,

even louder than before!

whoo, whoo,
drowsy barn owl speaks.

kerrrrrr-ick,
the old farmhouse squeaks.

a-woooo,

howls coyote, miles from the house.

Up goes the window.

"what was THAT?" wonders Mouse.

**crrr-oak!
crrr-oak!**
bullfrog sings through the thickets.

squeeeal,
rat-tat-tat!
blows the old screen door.
tip-tap!
tip-tap!
hound dog's tail beats the floor.

Wwwwwhooooossssshhhhh!

sings the breeze, through the trees.

**snort!
bloop-bloop-bloop!**
that's Granddad's snore.

**snort!
bloop-bloop-
bloop!**
even louder than before!

whoo! whoo!
drowsy barn owl speaks.

kerrrrrr-ick!
the old farmhouse squeaks.

a-woooo!

howls coyote,
miles from the house.

Up goes the window.

"what was
THAT?" wonders Mouse.

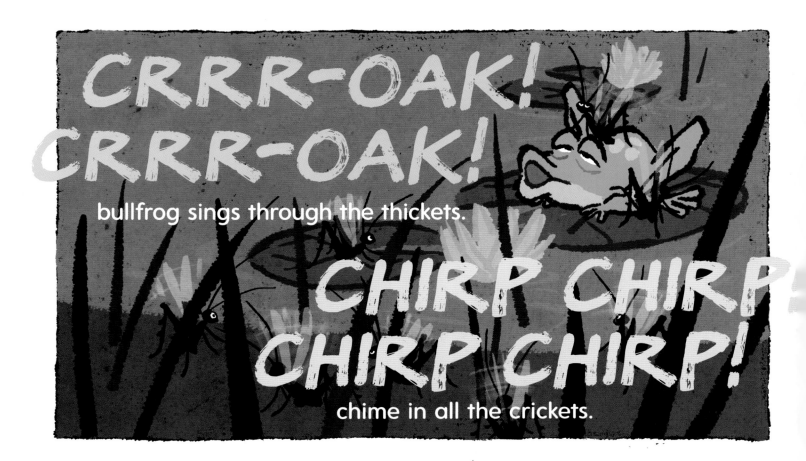

CRRR-OAK! CRRR-OAK!
bullfrog sings through the thickets.

CHIRP CHIRP! CHIRP CHIRP!
chime in all the crickets.

SQUEEEAL, RAT-TAT-TAT!
blows the old screen door.

TIP-TAP! TIP-TAP!
hound dog's tail beats the floor.

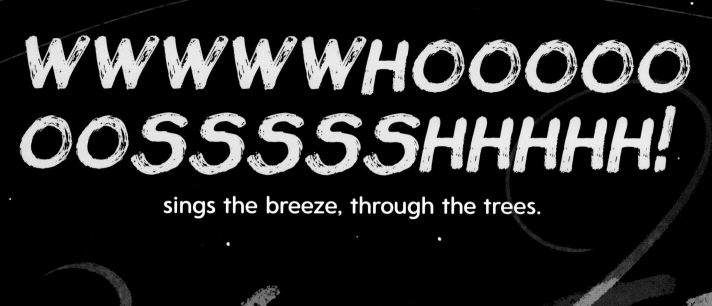

WWWWWHOOOOO OOSSSSSSHHHHH!

sings the breeze, through the trees.

SNORT! BLOOP-BLOOP-BLOOP-BLOOP!

that's Granddad's snore.

SNORT! BLOOP-BLOOP-BLOOP-BLOOP!

even louder than before!

WHOO?! WHOO?!

drowsy barn owl speaks.

KERRRR RR-ICK!

the old farmhouse squeaks.

WOOOOO!

howls coyote, miles from the house.

Up goes the window—

"BE QUIET!!! I'M TRYING TO SLEEP!"

bellows Mouse.

shah,
shah,
shah,

the moths brush against the light.

A *click!* turns the lamp off.

Now there's nothing but the night.

It's *soooo* quiet.

For West Virginia, my family, and my memories.

**For Melissa Manlove, who patiently helped me
write this song—and so, so many others.
And for Faith, for bringing it all together. —S. D. R.**

For Stacey, Eli, and Elinor. —T. F.

Library of Congress Cataloging-in-Publication Data:
Names: Rinker, Sherri Duskey, author. | Fucile, Tony, illustrator.
Title: It's so quiet / by Sherri Duskey Rinker, illustrated by Tony Fucile.
Other titles: It is so quiet
Description: San Francisco, California : Chronicle Books LLC, [2021] | ?2021
    | Summary: Little mouse cannot sleep because it is too quiet—but when he
    really listens he finds tonight is full of all sorts of sounds, so many
    if fact that it is too noisy to sleep.
Identifiers: LCCN 2015048856 | ISBN 9781452145440 (alk. paper)
Subjects: LCSH: Mice—Juvenile fiction. | Sleep—Juvenile fiction. |
    Sounds—Juvenile fiction. | Stories in rhyme. | CYAC: Stories in rhyme. |
    Bedtime—Fiction. | Sleep—Fiction. | Sounds—Fiction. | Mice—Fiction.
Classification: LCC PZ8.3.R4598 It 2021 | DDC 813.6—dc23 LC record
available at http://lccn.loc.gov/2015048856

Manufactured in China.

Design by Jennifer Tolo Pierce.
Typeset in Rodger and Plz Print Brush.
The illustrations in this book were rendered digitally.

10 9 8 7 6 5 4 3 2

Chronicle Books LLC
680 Second Street
San Francisco, California 94107

Chronicle Books—we see things differently. Become part of our community
at www.chroniclekids.com.